YOUR FRONT-ROW SEAT TO THE 1992 WINTER OLYMPICS!

This complete guide will take you through the Games from the selection of the teams to the final scoring procedures. Your favorite sports such as skiing and figure skating are profiled here along with the new "demonstration" sports such as curling and freestyle skiing.

Each winter sport has an exciting and colorful history. Now see how the sport developed to the modern, high-tech competition of today's Games and learn how the athletes prepare for each event.

The competition will be tough. American athletes are among the best in the world, but who will take the gold?

GOING FOR THE GOLD

MEDAL HOPEFULS FOR WINTER '92

DANIEL AND SUSAN COHEN

AN ARCHWAY PAPERBACK
Published by POCKET BOOKS
New York   London   Toronto   Sydney   Tokyo   Singapore

AN ARCHWAY PAPERBACK *Original*

An Archway Paperback published by
POCKET BOOKS, a division of Simon & Schuster Inc.
1230 Avenue of the Americas, New York, NY 10020

ISBN: 0-671-75418-1

First Archway Paperback printing January 1992

10 9 8 7 6 5 4 3 2 1

Cover photos by Dave Black Photography

Printed in the U.S.A.

IL 5+

CONTENTS

1. Winter Games   1
2. The Albertville Games   6
3. Television   10
4. Speed Skating   14
5. Figure Skating   26
6. Ice Hockey   43
7. Cross-Country Skiing   54
8. Ski Jumping   60
9. Nordic Combined   66
10. Alpine Skiing   69
11. Bobsled   79
12. Luge   94
13. Biathlon   109
14. Demonstration Sports   117
    Curling   118
    Speed Skiing   123
    Freestyle Skiing   126

GOING FOR THE
GOLD

1

WINTER GAMES

Ancient Greeks held religious festivals in honor of their gods, and athletic contests were often part of these festivals. One of the largest festivals was held once every four years in honor of the god Zeus at the valley of Olympus. The festival became known throughout Greece as the Olympiad, or the Olympic Games. So important did the Games become that wars were put on hold during these times. The Games became a symbol of peace and unity to the divided and often warring Greeks. Even after Greece was no longer a powerful nation, the Games were continued, well into the Roman era.

In modern times these ancient contests became an obsession to a French nobleman, Baron Pierre de Coubertin. He wanted to revive the Games and the Olympic spirit of peace and unity. With the support of some of

Opening ceremonies (Photo © Dave Black)

Europe's royalty and a Greek millionaire, he initiated the first modern Olympic Games in Athens in 1896.

The early history of the modern Olympics was not without problems. Politics and poor planning very nearly killed the Olympic movement. It wasn't until the Olympics went to Stockholm, Sweden, in 1912 that people really saw how great the Games could be. The next Olympics were scheduled to be held in Berlin in 1916 by which time the First World War was raging. The games were canceled because of the war. The Olympics began again after the war, but were canceled once again by the Second World War in 1940.

The Games were started up again after the conflict ended. Since that time they have been rocked by political unrest and a variety of disputes over such things as professionalism and the use of drugs. Despite all the well-publicized problems, the Olympics have continued to grow. The Olympics today are without doubt the largest and most prestigious sporting event in the world.

The early modern Olympics concentrated on events such as track and field, swimming, and other warm-weather sports. Winter sports such as figure skating and ice hockey, when they could be held on artificial ice, were presented at some of the early Olympics as "special events." But there was no way that skiing or bobsledding could be performed in the summer.

In 1924 an Olympics especially designed for winter sports was put on in the French ski resort of Chamonix. The first Winter Games were limited. There were only seven events, and just one of these, figure skating, included a women's competition. Thirteen nations, with a total of 294 competitors took part. Small as they were, the Chamonix Games were considered a success, and the next Winter Games at the Swiss winter resort of Saint Moritz were larger.

The Winter Games grew steadily until World War II forced the cancellation of the 1940 and 1944 contests. Like the Summer Games, they began again after the war, and they have continued to grow, both in number of participants and in popularity. The Winter Games are still much smaller than the Summer Games because there are fewer winter sports. Despite an occasional oddity, like a bobsled team from the tropical island of Jamaica, nations without snow and ice rarely send teams.

The fact that the Winter Games are smaller doesn't mean they are in any way inferior to the Summer Games. Events such as bobsledding and speed skating are faster than any summer sports. Nordic combined is more physically demanding, figure skating is more graceful, and a number of events such as the

4

Alpine downhill are more dangerous. All of these events demand great nerve as well as great skill.

Usually the Winter Olympics are held in places where there are limited and therefore expensive accommodations, so there have been relatively few spectators. But television—through which most of the world experiences the Olympics, both summer and winter—is exceptionally good at conveying the excitement of most of the winter events. No Olympic event looks more thrilling and beautiful on television than figure skating. In fact, for many events it is better to see the action on TV than to stand out in the cold and watch it in person.

Weather plays a larger part in the Winter Games than in the summer contests, and it makes them somewhat unpredictable—and therefore extremely interesting.

For more information:

United States Olympic Committee
1750 Boulder Street
Colorado Springs, CO 80909
(719) 578-4654

2

THE
ALBERTVILLE
GAMES

Countries and cities compete for the privilege
of hosting the Olympics just as fiercely as the
athletes compete against one another in the
Games themselves. Cities have built gigantic
stadiums and whole villages to accommodate
the Olympics. That's fine for the Summer
Games. But no city or country can build mountains and provide snow, which are absolutely
essential for the Winter Games. The number
of potential sites for the Winter Olympics is
rather limited, then, and places such as Saint
Moritz, Switzerland; Innsbruck, Austria; and
Lake Placid, New York, have all hosted the
Winter Games more than once.

Most Winter Games have been held in European winter resort areas. The sixteenth Winter
Olympics, which will take place from Febru-

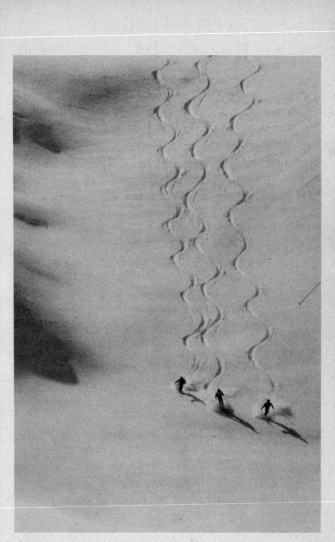

Skiing in the French Alps (French Government Tourist Office)

ary 6 to February 23, 1992, will continue in this tradition. The center for the Games will be the small city of Albertville in the French Alps. Albertville will be the site of the opening and closing ceremonies and the skating events. Other events will be held at lovely sites scattered throughout the surrounding mountains. The whole area is world famous for its winter resorts such as Val-d'Isère and Tignes. Many of these resorts already have Olympic-quality facilities available and will be familiar to many of the world-class athletes who compete in the Games.

The sixteenth Winter Olympic Games are expected to attract some 1,500 athletes from around the world. Fifty-five gold medals will be awarded.

The Albertville Games will be the last Winter Olympics to be held in the same year as the Summer Games. The International Olympic Committee has decided that it is too difficult to manage the two events so close to each other. It was easier to change the timing for the smaller Winter Games. The seventeenth Winter Games will be held two years after the sixteenth Games, in 1994, in Lillehammer, Norway. After that, the Winter Games will revert to a four-year schedule so that they'll always take place in the years between the Summer Games.

Tignes, one of the sites for the Winter Games (French Government Tourist Office)

3

TELEVISION

Approximately 35,000 people will be able to find seats in the stadium at Albertville to watch the opening and closing ceremonies at the Olympics. The Ice Hall in which the popular figure skating events will be held has a seating capacity of 9,000, and there will never be enough tickets available. French tourism officials estimate, perhaps optimistically, that nearly a million people will jam the hotels and resorts around Albertville to see at least a small part of the sixteenth Winter Games.

Among the visitors will be several thousand television reporters and technicians, and through their efforts an estimated two *billion* people worldwide will see the games. People living in countries where there is no snow will watch breathlessly as skiers plunge down the snow-covered Bellevarde face at Val-d'Isère.

Back in the nineteenth century when Baron Pierre de Coubertin revived the Olympics, he envisioned it as a way of bringing the world together. It hasn't quite worked out that way, as two world wars and a lot of political wrangling have shown. At first the Olympics were only for rich men. Poor people didn't have the money to participate or attend the games as spectators.

Television has, to a remarkable degree, changed all that. It has made the Olympics a truly international event. For sixteen days in February 1992 people all over the world, rich and poor, will be seated in front of their TV sets to watch the Winter Games at Albertville. And the dream to compete in an Olympic sport will be born in many young people, not from observing the sport itself, but from seeing it on television.

In the United States the Winter Games will be presented on CBS, which plans almost 120 hours of coverage between February 8 and February 23. That will be the most coverage ever for any Winter Games on network television. The previous high was 94.5 hours in 1988.

CBS has not broadcast the Olympics for thirty-two years, not since 1960. CBS was the first U.S. network to broadcast the Olympic Games when it covered the 1960 Winter Games in Squaw Valley, California, and the Summer Games in Rome, Italy. The Olympics were not such a big deal on television then. There were only fifteen hours of coverage on the Winter Games and twenty on the Summer Games.

11

The times of Olympic coverage will vary from day to day during the Games, but in general there will be a couple of hours in the morning (7:00 A.M. to 9:00 A.M. Eastern Standard Time), and prime time coverage each weekday evening (8:00 P.M. to 11:00 P.M. Eastern Standard Time). There will also be a half-hour update each weekday afternoon, and a one-hour late-night wrap-up. On weekends there will be several hours of afternoon coverage. You'll be able to check your local listings to find exact times and to see what events are being broadcast.

In addition to the CBS coverage, Turner Broadcasting System (TBS), a cable network, will broadcast an additional fifty hours of Olympic coverage on weekday afternoons from 1:00 P.M. to 6:00 P.M., and from 6:00 P.M. to 7:00 P.M. on weekends. The cable coverage will give viewers a chance to see some of the lesser known Olympic events—those not usually seen on network TV.

The U.S. television coverage of the Albertville Olympics will be absolutely unprecedented. It will give the viewers a chance to see not only the glamorous events such as figure skating and men's downhill but also many sports such as luge and Nordic combined, which you may never have heard of.

This may be one of your last chances to watch the Olympics on free TV. There are plans to put many of the events at the 1992

Summer Games on pay-per-view television. Rights to the 1994 Winter Games at Lillehammer, Norway, have also been acquired by CBS and TBS, but after that, the Winter Games may be pay-per-view as well.

The anchors for the CBS coverage will be familiar to many. Co-anchors for the prime time coverage will be sports announcer Tim McCarver and Paula Zahn from the CBS program "This Morning." Weekend daytime coverage will be hosted by Jim Nantz and Andrea Joyce of CBS sports. Harry Smith of "This Morning" and Greg Gumbel from the sports department will handle the weekday morning programs, and Pat O'Brien, another sports reporter, will host the late-night shows.

Scott Hamilton, 1984 Olympic figure skating gold medalist, will be lead analyst for the skating coverage. He will be joined by Katarina Witt, gold medalist in 1984 and 1988. The announcer for the figure skating competition, which will undoubtedly be the highlight of the CBS coverage, will be veteran sportscaster Verne Lundquist.

There's going to be a lot to see in the 1992 Winter Olympics, but to really enjoy what's on, you should understand all of the sports, how they began and how they are scored. Also it would be good to know what and whom to watch for at Albertville. The aim of this book is to supply this information.

4

SPEED
SKATING

History

First came skiing. Then at some point—no
one knows when, but it was thousands of
years ago—skis were shortened and used to
cross ice rather than snow. Thus was born a
very primitive type of skate. In the beginning
skaters, like skiers, had to push themselves
along with poles. The earliest skates were made
of bone, then later polished wood. There may
have been iron skates as early as A.D. 200,
though for centuries most skaters continued to
use bone or wooden skates. At first skating was
simply a means of traveling over ice. But people
have a way of making games out of their means
of transportation and their tools.

Skating has its own patron saint. In 1395 a
Dutch girl by the name of Lidwina fell and was
injured while skating with friends. Complica-

tions from the injury made her an invalid, and she was in constant pain. She was a deeply religious young woman and began having visions. Those who visited her claimed that miracles took place in her presence. After she died, a shrine was built over her grave, where the devout came to pray. In 1891 she was canonized and became the patron saint of skating.

It was in Lidwina's native Holland that skating really developed. Paintings from the fifteenth century show people on the frozen lakes and canals enjoying the sport on ironclad wooden skates.

It wasn't until 1542 that a Scottish innovator made the first pair of all-metal skates. With them skating as an organized sport really began. By the eighteenth century, skating clubs had been organized all over Europe. The first recorded speed skating race took place in England over a distance of fifteen miles on February 4, 1763. In those early races most of the participants were laborers whose daily work gave them practice in skating over frozen canals. It was a rugged sport. There were big cash prizes for winners. The aristocrats stood alongside the frozen lakes to watch and to bet heavily on the outcome.

By the middle of the nineteenth century speed skating dominated ice sports in Holland and was considered the national sport. Perhaps because of stories like *Hans Brinker and the Silver Skates*, Holland is still thought of as the birthplace of speed skating. In fact, the United States played a significant role in the history of the sport. Scottish settlers brought speed skating to the New World and made it popular in the North American colonies. However, the first speed skating championship was not held on American soil until 1889.

Iron skates were heavy, and the blades lost their sharp edge after a few hours of even casual skating. Then in 1850 E. W. Bushnell of Philadelphia started to make all-steel skates. They were light, strong, and maintained their sharp edges during months of hard use.

The new steel skates turned skating into a popular craze, particularly in America. As indoor rinks and artificial ice became more popular than frozen ponds and canals, racing became more standardized. Some speed skating races are still held outdoors, but most international competitions are skated on indoor tracks, and most world records are set at just a handful of these indoor facilities.

Modern Speed Skating

The object of speed skating today is exactly the same as it has been since the sport began—to skate faster than the other racers. There are two basic types of races. The most familiar is the long track, which is skated on a 4000-meter oval track. There are races of different lengths, from 500 meters to 10,000 meters for men and from 500 meters to 5,000 meters for women.

The races are conducted in pairs, but the athletes are racing the clock, not one another. Winning in a pair does not mean winning the event. To be the winner of the event, the skater must have the fastest time at the end of a group, or heat. There can be a dozen or more pairs in a group. Speed skaters usually prefer to skate with the fastest skater possible. The faster the other person, the faster both times are likely to be.

The distance around the outer edge of a speed skating track is longer than the distance around the inside edge. To make sure that both skaters race the same distance, staggered starts are sometimes used.

In order to make conditions for each racer as nearly equal as possible, skaters regularly change lanes. After the first lap, or trip around the rink, the skaters change lanes each time they complete another lap. In other words, each racer skates once around the inner track, then once around the outer, alternating until the conclusion of the event. Crossovers are always done at the same point on the track, the backstretch. The skater leaving the outer lane on the backstretch first is considered to have the right-of-way and may cross into the inner lane first.

In shorter races, skaters simply go flat out

as fast as they can, just as a runner does during a sprint. But longer races make it necessary for the racer to conserve as much energy as possible. During a long race a skater will rest an arm on his or her back. That saves the energy that would otherwise be used pumping the arm back and forth. It also gives the skater a more aerodynamic shape and cuts wind resistance.

The Albertville Olympics will see the first medal competition in what is called short track speed skating. This was a demonstration event during the 1988 Games in Calgary, Canada. It is skated on a 111-meter track. For the spectator the big difference is that the competitors race in "pack style," or "track style." The racers really are competing against one another. A good deal more strategy is required in this sort of race. It is also a very exciting sport to watch. There will be two short track events for men, the 1,000-meter and the 5,000-meter relay, and two for women, the 500-meter and the 3,000-meter relay. Speed skating events were held as track-style races in the Lake Placid Olympics in 1932. This method, with five or six men on the track at the same time, was called "North American Rules." It so outraged European competitors that some refused to participate. The system of two competitors against the clock was reinstated at the next Olympics and was used exclusively in

Olympic and international competition until the introduction of short track skating.

How fast do speed skaters go? An official publication of the U.S. International Speedskating Association says that World and American record holder Nick Thometz's best time for the 500-meter sprint is just over 36 seconds: "Remember, we are talking about a distance roughly equal to that of five football fields, or over one-quarter mile, and starting from a dead stop on an icy surface. Covering the 500-meter distance in 36 seconds roughly translates to just under 40 miles an hour. The fastest a human being has ever run is just over 22 miles an hour for a short distance. Horses can obviously beat men who are skating, but perhaps not by as much as you might imagine. The fastest a horse has ever been clocked for distances comparable to 1,000 meters is about 40 miles an hour. Obviously, speed skating is the fastest an individual can move under his or her own power. It certainly is impressive."

Technology has played a part in improving speed skating, not only in the construction of rinks but also in the designing of skates and even uniforms. Racing skates have extra-long blades to allow for a longer glide. As long as the glide lasts, the racer moves forward. Long blades keep the glide going without loss of speed. Metal-tempering technology, sharpening techniques and tools, and modern boot

19

design have contributed to the lessening of wind drag and weight.

Speed skating uniforms, like the uniforms used in many other winter sports, are designed to minimize air resistance. They are one-piece garments that cover the athlete from head to toe. The uniforms are custom made of shiny nylon and are worn skintight to cut air resistance. The nylon is so dense that air rushes over its surface, rather than dragging, as it does on other fabrics. The stretchability of these uniforms allows the athlete complete freedom of movement. The uniforms alone can save a competitor tenths of seconds in races that are often won by hundredths of seconds.

The Olympics

Speed skating has been part of the Winter Games from the start. There were men's races at the 1924 games at Chamonix. The first gold medal winner at the Winter Games was American Charles Jewtraw from Lake Placid, New York, who won in the 500-meter race. Women's races had been demonstration sports at several Olympics, but didn't become official medal-awarding sports until 1960. Though it is not really a popular winter sport in America, speed skating is one in which Americans have done very well. In fact, the United States has collected more medals at the Winter Games in speed skating than in any other sport.

Before the speed skating events were moved indoors, weather could severely affect the outcome. For example, in the 1968 Games American Richard "Terry" McDermott was the clear favorite. But he had the bad luck of skating in the last of twenty-four pairs. By that time the sun had so badly melted the ice that his time was not so good as expected. It was good enough to earn him second place, though. Winner Erhard Keller of Germany said of McDermott, "What he did today was just sheer guts. If he had started in the earlier heats when the ice was still good, I'd have lost. It's as simple as that." In 1928, because the ice was melting, the 10,000-meter race was actually canceled after seven of the ten entrants had completed their heats.

The greatest of all American Olympic speed skaters, and quite possibly the greatest speed skater, period, was Eric Heiden. He started in pack-style skating and at the age of seventeen had appeared in the 1976 Olympics where his performance was not particularly impressive. But over the next few years he improved dramatically and became something of a hero, not in the United States, but in Norway and Holland where speed skating is taken seriously. When he entered the 1980 Olympics at Lake Placid he was a clear favorite in all five men's speed skating events. He did not disappoint his admirers. He won five individual gold medals and set four Olympic records, a feat that has never been equaled. (In the Summer Games swimmer Mark Spitz won seven gold medals, but three were in relay events).

Eric Heiden's feat could not be ignored, even in the United States, which was traditionally indifferent to speed skating. Heiden became an instant celebrity. It wasn't a role that he was comfortable with, so he retired from speed skating to take up bicycle racing. "Maybe if things had stayed the way they were," he said, "and I could still be obscure in an obscure sport, I might want to keep skating. I really liked it best when I was a nobody."

Eric's younger sister, Beth, was also an Olympic-class speed skater. She took a bronze in the women's 3,000-meter race in 1980.

The most dramatic, tragic, and courageous figure at the 1988 Calgary Olympics was American speed skater Dan Jansen. Jansen was favored to win medals in both the 500- and 1,000-meter races. But Jansen knew that his sister was dying of leukemia. On the morning when he was scheduled to skate in the 500-meter race, the phone call came that she had just died. That afternoon he fell on the ice at the first turn. World-class skaters almost never fall in competition. Jansen couldn't remember the last time he had fallen.

Four days later in the 1,000-meter race Jansen was again the favorite. Again he fell, this time after having skated the fastest 600 meters through the first four pairs.

"I couldn't believe it," he said. Neither could anyone else. Jansen became the story of the 1988 Olympics, but it was not the sort of attention that he wanted or needed.

Jansen, however, did not give up. He has continued in competition and has been skating well. He is considered the strongest male skater on the U.S. Olympic team and will once again try for that elusive medal in the Albertville Games. His greatest challenge may well be in dealing with the media circus and the questions that will be raised because of what happened at Calgary.

Almost lost in all the publicity that surrounded Jansen's tragedy was the performance of Bonnie Blair who won the gold in the women's 500-meter race and a bronze in the 1,000. She will also be at Albertville, and she is believed to have a good chance of repeating her winning performance in the 500-meter race.

What to Watch For

The obvious human-interest story of these Winter Games will be Dan Jansen, but try to overlook the hype and concentrate on his performance. That's what Jansen will be trying to do. And don't forget about Bonnie Blair.

Also make an effort to catch the short track

U.S. speed skater Bonnie Blair (Photo by Nancie Battaglia)

events. It is always more exciting to see athletes competing against one another than against the clock, as in most speed skating events.

For more information:

Sean Callahan
United States International Speedskating
    Association
2005 North 84th Street
Wauwatosa, WI 53226
(414) 475-7465

5

FIGURE SKATING

History

Using skates as a means of getting across the ice is, as we have said, an ancient practice. By the early nineteenth century this practical means of locomotion had evolved into a recreational activity, though. People skated simply because they enjoyed it, not because they had to get anywhere. With the development of steel skates it became possible to make tightly controlled turns on the ice. As the skater turned, the blades inscribed certain forms or figures on the ice. The most familiar was the figure eight. That's where the term *figure* skating came from. Combinations of various turns developed, and the turns became increasingly complex. The style and manner in which these turns were made became standardized, and soon competitions were organized.

Figure skating really began in Europe, but an American ballet master named Jackson Haines, who was born in New York City in 1840, profoundly influenced the development of the sport. Just before the Civil War, a skating craze, accompanied by a dancing craze, swept America, and during this time Haines leapt into the limelight with a daring combination of skating and dance. Figure skating had developed a stiff, rigid style, and Haines's free and expressive performances were frowned upon, if not actually condemned. He did manage to win a championship in America, but the continued cool reception given to him prompted him to leave for Europe.

He skated in England, but his reception there was just as cool as it had been in America. When he skated in Vienna, Austria, however, he became a huge success. Vienna was the home of the graceful Viennese waltz. Haines remained in Europe for eleven years and developed what was called the "international style of figure skating." He planned to return to America but died in 1875 before coming home. He caught pneumonia during a blizzard he encountered while traveling by sled from Saint Petersburg, Russia, to Stockholm, Sweden.

Haines, an American, is known as "the father of figure skating," though his style didn't really reach America until the early years of the twentieth century. When it did,

27

it took very firm root. The United States has been one of the leaders in world figure skating for most of this century.

The Events

In Olympic figure skating competition there are three basic events: the singles, with events for both men and women; the pairs; and ice dance. In all the events skaters are required to appear twice, first in a short program in which they must perform certain basic moves, and then in a long program, which also contains required moves, but in which the skaters are given more freedom. A combined score from the long and short programs makes up each skater's final score, but the long program is given much more weight than the short program.

A major change in the 1992 Games is that the school figures—tracing very precise patterns in the ice—have been eliminated. These figures were the activity that gave figure skating its name, and until 1968 these compulsory figures counted for 60 percent of each competitor's total score. This percentage was gradually reduced, and by 1990 the figures had been eliminated entirely in world competition. The 1992 Winter Games will be the first Olympics without the figures.

All sports evolve, and there are many reasons why the school figures were dropped. One of the main reasons had to be television. Technically, skating school figures was a precise and difficult activity. Except for the truly knowledgeable, it wasn't much to look at, though, particularly when compared to the grace and beauty of the free skating performances. In major skating competitions like the Olympics the compulsory figures competition was rarely even shown on TV. Viewers were often puzzled and even angered when a skater who had given a terrific free skating performance finished behind an inferior free skater who had been near perfect in the figures. Skating had changed from an activity that attracted a relatively small audience to a major spectator sport. Top skaters became celebrities and went on to careers as professional skaters. Professionals never do school figures. The public wanted free skating because it was beautiful to watch, and ultimately the public got what it wanted.

Unlike a race, where the winner is the one who crosses the finish line first, in figure skating the winner is not so easy to determine. Winners are decided upon by a group of judges. In the Olympics there are nine judges, each from a different country. Skaters are awarded from 0 to 6 points on technical merit and artistic impression. Overall rankings are determined on the basis of a complicated mathematical formula.

There are rules in judging. A fall or a failure to perform a required maneuver will result in specific point deductions, but in the end the decisions the judges make are just that, matters of judgment. Often the scores awarded by judges vary greatly, and there are suspicions that more than a difference of opinion is involved. A judge from the same country as the skater being considered tends to give that skater more points. High and low scores are thrown out, though, to avoid extreme bias one way or the other. Certain styles or moves tend to be favored by certain judges. A style that is considered radical and is penalized one year may get high marks the next. There is almost always some controversy over the results in the Olympic figure skating events. Figure skating isn't the only Olympic sport in which judging controversies erupt, but it is such a popular sport that any controversy tends to be magnified.

The Olympics

Figure skating has been part of the Olympics since the first Winter Games. It is an event in which the United States has historically been a top contender, particularly in individual competitions. But it was a Norwegian girl by the name of Sonja Henie who became figure skating's first and greatest star. Figure skating is one of the very few Olympic sports in which women generally become more famous than men.

Sonja Henie first appeared in the 1924 Olympics, when she was only eleven years old, and she placed eighth. By 1928 she was regarded as the best woman figure skater in the world, and she easily took the gold medal. Her domination was even more complete in the 1932 Winter Games. By 1936 she was so famous that she had to have police protection wherever she went. Henie announced that she would end her amateur career after the 1936 world championships, to be held one week after the Olympics. She wanted to finish out her amateur career with wins, and she felt a great deal of pressure on her. Her free skating performance was not up to her usual standard, but it was good enough for another gold medal. She then went on to win her tenth straight world championship.

After ending her competitive career, Sonja Henie became a movie star. She made ten enormously successful motion pictures that featured her skating. In addition, she was a very astute businesswoman. She invested her money wisely and became enormously wealthy.

During the 1950s the two best women figure skaters in the world were Americans Tenley Albright and Carol Heiss. In 1956 Albright, a surgeon's daughter, severely cut her ankle in practice two weeks before the Olympics. Her father rushed to Cortina, Italy, where the Olympics were being held, and treated the injury. Albright then went on to win the gold medal. After the Olympics she retired from skating and went to Harvard Medical School. She became a surgeon herself and specializes in sports injuries.

Heiss had come in second to Albright at Cortina in 1956. That year her mother died of cancer, and Heiss made a vow to win the Olympic Gold Medal in her honor. That she did at Squaw Valley in 1960. She is now a top figure skating coach.

The next U.S. woman to win the gold was the beautiful and elegant Peggy Fleming. She won easily at the Winter Games in Grenoble, France, in 1968, and was the only U.S. gold medal winner in those games. Peggy Fleming is still seen frequently on television as a commentator on figure skating events. In 1976 the winner was Dorothy Hamill. Though she lacked Fleming's effortless grace, she won easily and became a darling of the American public. By 1976 the Winter Games had become a major television event.

In 1972 and again in 1980 winners in the school figures went on to take gold medals, although they did poorly in the free skating. In 1972 Beatrix Schuba built up a huge lead in the figures and coasted to victory in spite of a seventh place finish in free skating. In 1980 Denise Biellmann of Switzerland was a

Peggy Fleming performing compulsory figures during the 1968 Olympics (Wide World Photo)

crowd favorite and turned in a stunning free skating performance, far outdistancing her rivals. But she had done poorly in the compulsories and didn't even get a medal.

Katarina Witt of East Germany took the gold in 1984 and again in 1988. This beautiful and poised performer became an international superstar and is frequently seen in televised ice-skating shows.

American men have also greatly influenced the sport. The man who changed figure skating the most was America's Richard Button. In 1948 the eighteen-year-old Harvard freshman was the first person to successfully complete a double axel jump in Olympic competition. In 1952 he introduced the even more difficult triple loop, which required him to make three complete revolutions in the air and come down smoothly. All the judges placed him far ahead of the other skaters. Dick Button went on to become a professional skater and is well known as a TV commentator on skating.

Other U.S. men to win gold medals were David Jenkins in 1960, Scott Hamilton in 1984, and Brian Boitano in 1988. Hamilton will be the TV commentator for skating in the 1992 games.

Since 1964 the pairs competition has been dominated by teams from the Soviet Union. Occasionally what happened outside the competition attracted as much attention as the per-

Soviet pairs skaters Usova and Zhulin (Photo by Ingrid Butt)

Soviet pairs skaters Mishkuteniok and Dmitriev (Photo by Ingrid Butt)

formance itself. In 1972 the heavily favored Soviet team of Irina Rodnina and Aleksei Ulanov had a well-publicized falling-out. Ulanov had become romantically involved with Lyudmila Smirnova of the number two USSR team. The competition became something of a soap opera, and after the long program Rodnina left the ice in tears. Despite the turmoil, Rodnina and Ulanov finished first, and Smirnova and her partner Andrei Surakin finished second, just as had been expected. Rodnina found a new partner, Aleksander Zaitsev, married him, and went on to win two more gold medals.

In 1980 it looked as though the American team of Randy Gardner and Tai Babilonia might really challenge the Soviets. But shortly before the Olympics Gardner was injured. He tried to compete but fell four times in the warm-ups, and the pair was forced to withdraw, a heartbreaking moment.

Ice dancing had been around longer than pairs skating, but it was not introduced as an Olympic event until 1976. The British pair, Jayne Torvill and Christopher Dean, brought the discipline to an entirely new level. In world competitions they earned the first perfect scores in the event's history. At Sarajevo, Yugoslavia, in 1984 they absolutely captivated the audience with their interpretation of Ravel's *Bolero*. They got across-the-board perfect

Kristi Yamaguchi (Photo © Dave Black)

scores for artistic impression. Torvill and Dean have now retired from competition, and no one expects to see their artistry matched for a very long time—if ever.

What to Watch For

World-class skaters will have had nearly two years to adjust to figure skating without school figures, so the change will probably not affect the outcome of the 1992 Games. The United States will be sending a strong team to the Games with an outside chance for a sweep in the women's event, a medal or two in the men's, and perhaps also a medal in pairs.

At the 1991 World Championships three Americans—Kristi Yamaguchi, Tonya Harding, and Nancy Ann Kerrigan—finished first, second, and third. But 1990 world champion American Jill Trenary may have the best shot at the gold. There will, however, be strong challenges from Japan and Canada. The women's singles competition promises to be one of the most exciting and unpredictable in many years. Some of the skaters may be attempting jumps never before tried by women in Olympic competition.

The United States is not so strong in the men's singles, but Todd Eldredge, who took a third in the 1991 World Championships is a definite contender for a medal. So is the brilliant but often erratic Chris Bowman. This one-time

Chris Bowman (Photos on Ice, Paul Harvath)

U.S. pairs skaters Natasha Kuchiki and Todd Sand (Photo © Dave Black)

child actor is one of the most flamboyant skaters around, and he is always fun to watch.

The United States has never been particularly strong in pairs, but Natasha Kuchiki and Todd Sand, who won the bronze medal at the 1991 World Championships, are given a chance to repeat their triumph and perhaps do even better at the Olympics.

For more information:

United States Figure Skating Association
20 First Street
Colorado Springs, CO 80906
(719) 635-5200

6

ICE HOCKEY

History

The origins of ice hockey are obscure. Many authorities believe that it grew out of a very ancient game, played on grass, that is now called field hockey. In field hockey, which is a sport in the Summer Games, the players use bent sticks to try to knock a ball into the opposing team's net. Others think that ice hockey originated in a game called bandy. The *Encyclopedia Britannica* has this to say about the game that has never quite outgrown its rather rowdy reputation:

> A bandy-type game, similar to ice hockey, was played in England as early as 1895. It was known as shinty (shinny or shinney) in Scotland and as ice hurling in Ireland and was a crude game played on frozen lakes and rivers with curved sticks (bandies) and a ball

(not a puck), with few rules and considerable bloodshed.

Whatever its origins, ice hockey certainly developed in Canada and spread to the northern United States in the late nineteenth and early twentieth centuries. It was taken up by college students and soon became an important winter game. By 1917 there were already professional hockey teams, and this profoundly affected Olympic hockey, which until the 1992 games had barred professional hockey players from competing.

Practically every sports fan is familiar with ice hockey, but it is professional hockey, not the amateur or college game, that people watch. Amateur hockey gets attention in North America only during Olympic years.

The rules for both professional and amateur hockey are essentially the same, but the fights and violence that are characteristic of the professional game are not tolerated in the Olympics.

The Olympics

Hockey was one of the original sports of the Winter Games. And for many years no country dominated a sport as completely as the Canadians dominated hockey. Ice hockey had become the national game of Canada, and for many years the Canadians dominated both amateur and professional hockey. From the beginning until 1952, Canadian ice hockey teams compiled an extraordinary Olympic record of thirty-seven wins, one loss, and three ties. In the forty-one games the Canadians played they scored 403 goals while allowing only 34 by their opponents. Canada would win games with scores like 20 to 0. In 1928 Olympic officials at Saint Moritz took a look at the Canadian team in practice and decided that they were so far superior to any other team that the competition would be a joke. So they devised an unusual system. Canada was advanced directly to the final round, and the other ten nations were divided into three pools. The three winners then joined Canada in the final round. There was some competition in the pools, but Canada won its three games 11–0, 14–0, and 13–0.

Canada's lone defeat during this period came in 1936 at the hands of Great Britain, and the defeat was a controversial one. Two of the British players were Canadians who had moved to Britain shortly before the Olympics. In fact, most of the British players had originally come from Canada. The International Ice Hockey Federation had voted to ban the two players from competing in the Olympics; however, they played anyway. No one is quite sure how they got away with it. Canada's undefeated streak was stopped at twenty, and

Olympic hockey (Photo by Nancie Battaglia)

as a result of the defeat the British team was able to win the gold, with Canada coming in second.

By the 1948 Games other teams had begun to give the Canadians a run. In the final game Canada had to beat Switzerland to take top honors. Since the games were being held in Switzerland, the crowd was very partisan. About five hundred Swiss perched on the cliffs and watched the game, pelting officials with snowballs whenever they disagreed with a call, which was frequently. It didn't do any good—the Canadians won 3–0.

In 1952 Canada won again, but the complete domination of the earlier years was gone. The United States played Canada to a 3–3 tie, but that was still good enough to give the Canadians the championship, for they had won all of their other games. The unheralded United States had played mighty Canada to a tie and surprised everyone. However, the U.S. team members were not popular with the spectators because of their rough style of play. Three U.S. players spent more time in the penalty box than all of the players on any of the other eight teams.

Hockey had been introduced into the Soviet Union and other Eastern European countries after World War II and was taken up with enormous enthusiasm. By the time the 1956 Winter Games were held, it was the Soviets, not the Canadians, who dominated world hockey. In 1956 the Soviet hockey team took its first gold medal, and the players impressed the crowd at Cortina, not only with their excellent play but with their clean style as well.

In the 1960 games at Squaw Valley the Soviets and Canadians were the favorites, but it was a lightly regarded U.S. squad that turned out to be the "team of destiny." The U.S. team beat the Soviets in front of a highly partisan and emotional crowd. The next day they went on to beat a tough team from Czechoslovakia to clinch the gold medal.

For the next twenty years Soviet hockey teams dominated international play, and the Olympics, until they ran into another U.S. team of destiny in 1980. Once again a lightly regarded U.S. team pulled off a come-from-behind victory over the heavily favored Soviets and ultimately skated away with the gold. The hard-fought 4–3 victory over the Soviets in front of a wildly emotional and nationalistic crowd at Lake Placid set off one of the most memorable demonstrations in the history of the Olympics. It was certainly the most emotional demonstration for U.S. athletes at any Olympiad. Moreover, by that time the Olympics had become a television event. The victory was brought into millions of U.S. homes, and the excitement was not limited to the few thousand fans who were able to see the game in person. In some respects the U.S. reaction really ran counter to the Olympic spirit. The

U.S. hockey team wins the gold medal in the 1980 Olympics (Wide World Photo)

Olympics are supposed to produce a feeling of international good will. But the U.S. victory over the USSR resulted in a burst of raw nationalism, with the crowd chanting "U.S.A., U.S.A.!" But there could be no doubting the genuineness of the feelings that the victory triggered.

For the United States, the victory over the Soviet hockey team in 1980 is probably the high point of Winter Olympic history. People barely remember that this was not the game that clinched the gold medal. After beating the Soviets, the team still had to play Finland. If they had lost, the Soviets would have won the tournament anyway.

The Finns were not going to roll over, and after two periods led 2–1. But the United States came on strong in the third period, and the final score was U.S.A. 4, Finland 2, a result that set off yet another emotional reaction from the crowd. When the Winter Olympics were held outside the United States, as they were in 1984 and 1988, the United States was unable to repeat its dramatic victories, and the Big Red Machine of the Soviet Union skated away with the gold medals. The U.S. teams received criticism, most of it unfair, for not being able to pull off another miracle.

What to Watch For

For years the United States and many other Western countries insisted that the Soviets and other Eastern European countries had an advantage in the Olympics. The communist states, they said, supported their athletes and teams and were able to field contestants who were, for all practical purposes, professionals. The rules requiring amateur status, however, prevented many Western athletes from getting the kind of commercial backing they needed to support themselves through their training. There can be a lot of argument about how valid this criticism was in many sports, but there is no doubt that it had a tremendous effect in ice hockey. Canada and the United States produce the best hockey players in the world, but they go, not to the Olympics, but directly into the ranks of the professional teams in the National Hockey League, which immediately disqualifies them from Olympic competition. In Canada and the United States ice hockey has always been more popular as a professional than as an amateur sport.

For the 1992 Olympics, however, the rules have been changed. For the first time professional hockey players will be allowed to play for their national teams. This is good news for the United States and Canada, whose top players have always been professionals and who have entered all prior Olympic competitions with essentially college all-star teams. However, the change may not be so dramatic. The Olympic competition takes place right in the middle of the NHL season. As we have already noted, professional hockey is far more important than Olympic competition in the United States and Canada. The professional teams are not going to allow their highly paid top players to take time out to skate in the Olympics.

According to Dave Peterson, coach of the U.S. Olympic squad, "In terms of having pro players on the team, it's not really a question of eligibility, it's a question of availability. Since the NHL schedule and the Winter Olympics both run at the same time, I don't expect to see a lot of NHL players on our team. But we have over one hundred American minor league pros and another hundred or so Americans playing in Europe, as well as a hundred collegians in our talent pool and some players in other situations who might be able to help us. Our Olympic team will involve some different combinations of players rather than simply the best college players, as we have had in the past."

Peterson is hoping some NHL teams will assign young players to the Olympic team, especially goaltenders and defensemen.

International politics may have an even greater effect on Olympic hockey than the rule change. Top players from the Soviet Union and other Eastern European countries have now joined the NHL, and therefore, like U.S. and Canadian pros, they will probably not be available to play for their countries. The defending gold medalists from the Soviet Union have lost three of their top players to the pros. In the past they would have remained with their national team. And no one can predict how the political upheaval in the Soviet Union will affect the performance of Soviet athletes in this or any other sport.

But the Soviets are still the team to beat. Czechoslovakia is also a favorite for a medal, as are a couple of the Scandinavian countries. The United States and Canada remain dark horses, but the teams are likely to be more closely matched than in the past. An exciting and unpredictable competition should be expected.

For more information:

Amateur Hockey Association of the
   United States, Inc.
2997 Broadmoor Valley Road
Colorado Springs, CO 80906
(719) 576-4990

7

CROSS-COUNTRY SKIING

History

Skiing is an ancient human activity. The oldest known ski—found in a bog in Sweden—goes back nearly forty-five centuries to about 2500 B.C., but the activity is doubtless a lot older than that. There is some evidence that pushes the date of the first skiers back to about 5000 B.C. For thousands of years, of course, it wasn't a sport but merely a means of getting around in the snow. Sleds probably came first, and when people saw that runners helped to move heavy loads across the snow, the idea of skis, which are really runners attached to human feet, would have followed naturally.

Skiing developed in the Scandinavian countries where there is lots of snow. Norwegian soldiers were on skis as early as A.D. 960. Within a couple of centuries Sweden had its own ski troops. As Scandinavians came to the United States they brought skiing with them. An official U.S. Ski Team publication notes that "A quick look at the records of the early ski competitions in the United States shows a list of winners that looks as if it were taken out of the Oslo or Stockholm phone book."

The Scandinavians introduced skiing to northern New England and the upper Midwest. Their influence spread as far as California. A famous early skier was John "Snowshoe" Thompson, the son of Norwegian immigrants who had brought him to the United States at the age of ten. For thirteen years Thompson delivered mail between Placerville, California, and Genoa, Nevada. When it snowed he used skis. Local settlers, who had never seen skis before, gave him the nickname "Snowshoe."

Nineteenth-century skis were long and heavy. They could be up to fourteen feet in length and were made from ash, pine, hickory, or oak. Some weighed up to twenty-five pounds each. At first, bindings were just a simple loop over the front part of the foot.

The Olympics

There were cross-country, or Nordic, ski races in the first Winter Games held in 1924, but only for men. Women's cross-country events did not begin to appear at the Olympics until the 1950s.

Olympic cross-country skiing was, and to a great extent still is, dominated by the Scandinavian countries and the Soviet Union. The greatest American cross-country skier was Bill Koch of Guilford, Vermont, known as "Billy Strongarms" by Europeans because of his powerful double-poling ability. In 1976 he stunned the skiing world by taking a silver medal in the 30-kilometer cross-country race. He is still the only American to have won an Olympic Nordic skiing medal. He became an instant celebrity, even in a country that didn't pay much attention to Olympic cross-country skiing. Vermonters are known for the brevity of their replies to questions, and Koch was no exception. When a reporter asked, "Have you lived in Vermont all your life?" he replied, "Not yet."

In spite of an upsurge of interest in cross-country skiing in America don't expect any U.S. medals in 1992. Cross-country is likely to be dominated by the traditional winners, the Scandinavians and the Soviets.

The Events

Cross-country skiing requires technique combined with tremendous strength and endurance. The races are run over a variety of distances from the 5-kilometer sprint to the 50-kilometer marathon. There are two skiing techniques: classical, which requires the conventional form of diagonal stride, and freestyle, which has no restrictions on technique and which uses a faster "skating" style. There are special boots, skis, wax, and poles for each technique. In major competitions 50 percent of the scheduled races are conducted in each technique. Most skiers will race using both techniques, and the fastest skiers in one are generally near the top in the other. The majority of race series give an overall award, which is the combined results of both styles.

The racecourses are laid out with a challenging combination of uphill, downhill, and rolling terrain. The machine-prepared trails are twelve to eighteen feet wide and have grooves set into them.

The races are difficult for the uninformed spectator to watch. Because the racers start one at a time at thirty-second intervals, the competitors are not really racing one another; they are merely racing the clock. The top skiers are on the course at the same time, and coaches along the track shout instructions to their athletes, letting them know how their competitors are doing.

Relay races are more exciting for the spectator, for skiers start at the same time and actually race against one another.

Cross-country skiing (Sports File, Graham Watson)

For more information:

United States Ski Team
P.O. Box 100
1500 Kearns Blvd.
Park City, UT 84060
(801) 649-9090

8

SKI JUMPING

History

Ski jumping began in the nineteenth century
after bindings had been developed to keep skis
from falling off during a jump. In the early
days it was pretty much a daredevil activity.
In America it became popular among such
sturdy fellows as gold miners and lumber-
jacks. The first recognized ski-jumping contest
was held in Trysil, Norway, in 1862. By the
start of the twentieth century ski jumping had
become a recognized international sport.

The Events

Ski jumping is one of the most spectacular
of all winter sports. It uses speed, power, and
the application of basic flight principles. In
fact, aerodynamics has become such an impor-

tant consideration in ski jumping that jumpers now speak of "floating," or "gliding."

Ski jumps consist of the inrun (the approach), the takeoff (the end of the inrun where the skier actually makes his jump), the landing hill, and the outrun (the flat area where the skier decelerates and stops).

In Olympic and world championship competition skiers jump on "normal hills" (formerly called 70-meter hills) and "large hills" (formerly called 90-meter hills). In international ski jumping, events are for men only.

Ski jumpers earn points based on the distance they jump and the form they exhibit during the jump, or "ride." These two elements are roughly equal in value in scoring. The winner in a contest is not necessarily the competitor who has had the longest jump. Distance points are calculated from a table which awards 60 points to a jump that reaches a predetermined spot on the landing hill. Points vary above and below 60, based on whether the jump was short of or beyond this spot.

In terms of form, a perfect jump would be awarded 60 points. Each of five judges may award up to 20 points for each jump, with the high and low marks thrown out. The style points of the remaining three judges are added together to determine the jumper's final score. Each contestant takes two jumps. In the Olympics there are team as well as individual medals.

Ski jumping (Photo by Nancie Battaglia)

The Olympics

Ski jumping was part of the first Winter Games held in 1924, but the winners of that event were not really decided until fifty years after it took place. Originally Thorleif Haug of Norway took the third-place bronze ski-jumping medal in addition to several other medals in other skiing events. However, in 1974 it was discovered that there had been an error in computing the scores. Haug, who had been dead for forty years, was demoted to fourth place and Anders Haugen a Norwegian-born member of the American team was awarded the bronze medal in a special ceremony in Oslo. He was eighty-three years old. He is still the only American to win a medal in Olympic ski jumping, no matter how belatedly.

Ski jumping has been dominated by the Europeans, though the Japanese swept the 70-meter event in the 1972 games held in Sapporo, Japan. The United States has never been strong, so don't expect any medals, or even high placements, in the Albertville Games. The event itself, however, is so spectacular that it attracts a great deal of attention, even in countries where ski jumping is not very popular.

The unlikely media star of the 1988 Calgary Olympics was a British ski jumper named Eddie Edwards, nicknamed "Eddie the Eagle." Ski jumping is virtually unknown as a sport in

Britain, where there is not a single ski jump hill on which to practice. In fact, Eddie the Eagle was a terrible jumper, and he finished dead last. But he had such an odd and engaging personality that the crowd and the TV audience loved him, and he became far better known than the winners of the event.

What to Watch For

Ski jumping appears to be as dangerous as any sport, and for the untrained athlete, it can be. But when conditions are right, ski jumping is safe and the incidence of injury is low. Contrary to the way it appears on television, jumpers are usually not more than ten feet in the air at any time, as their flight curve follows the curve of the hill. In the event of a fall, the athlete normally slides along the landing hill and then harmlessly onto the flat. Strong winds or exceptionally icy conditions can present enormous problems for jumpers, and competitors have sometimes been blown off the landing or turned over in the air. Officials will be watching the weather very closely, as ski-jumping events are often postponed.

In ski jumping, remember, style as well as distance counts. Look for the competitors who appear steady and controlled and who can make smooth landings. Back in 1928 the longest jump of the day was recorded by defending champion Jacob Tulin Thams of Norway. But he fell badly when he reached the ground, and the loss of style points dropped him to twenty-eighth place.

For more information:

United States Ski Team
P.O. Box 100
1500 Kearns Blvd.
Park City, UT 84060
(801) 649-9090

9

NORDIC COMBINED

In Nordic combined the athlete must compete in two events—ski jumping and a cross-country ski race. This is generally regarded as one of the most difficult combinations of athletic events in winter sports. While cross-country skiing is an endurance event, jumping is a speed and power event, and the athlete must develop qualities that are physically in opposition to each other. There are relatively few competitors in this sport, and in the United States it is virtually unknown, except among the hardy few.

The event has been part of the Olympics since the Winter Games began. It has usually been won by Scandinavians, most often Norwegians. However, the greatest Olympic competitor in this event was Ulrich Wehling of what was then East Germany. He won the gold medal in 1972, 1976, and 1980 and became

Joe Holland competing in Nordic combined (Photo by Nancie Battaglia)

the first man to win three consecutive gold medals in the same individual winter event.

Distances in the Olympic Nordic combined have varied somewhat over the years. At present the jump is on the normal, or 70-meter, hill and the cross-country race is 15 kilometers. In addition to individual medals there is also a team competition, in which the members compete in individual jumping and a team cross-country relay.

For more information:

United States Ski Team
P.O. Box 100
1500 Kearns Blvd.
Park City, UT 84060
(801) 649-9090

10

ALPINE SKIING

History

In the early days all skiing was what we now
call Nordic, or cross-country. The idea of skiing down a hill just for the fun of it was a
relatively late development in the history of
this ancient activity. The first downhill race
was held in Montana, Switzerland, in 1911. It
was organized by an Englishman, Arnold
Lunn, who also devised the other major downhill event, the slalom, in 1922. He was the
main force in obtaining Olympic recognition
for Alpine, or downhill, skiing in 1936, though
the first medal-awarding events did not appear
in the Winter Games until 1948 at Saint
Moritz.

Alpine skiing has certainly caught on with
the public now. Alpine skiing had already
become popular in Europe, and it began to be

Alpine skiing (Photo © Dave Black)

a popular sport in the United States during the Great Depression of the 1930s. The beginnings were humble. The owners of an inn in Vermont leased a hillside for ten dollars and installed a rope tow, powered by a Model-A engine: the car was jacked up and the rope went around one of the tire rims. In 1934 Averell Harriman, who owned the Union Pacific Railroad, sent an Austrian nobleman to scout prospective ski sites that might attract skiers along his rail line. A few years later Harriman opened Sun Valley with a chairlift designed by a railroad engineer based on a banana carrier he had helped build in South America. World War II also provided to boost to the sport. Many servicemen who had been given a chance to ski at some of the famous resorts in Europe came back filled with stories of the wonder of the sport. The American public was anxious for some winter fun after the sacrifices of the war years. Skiing provided it. The popularity of skiing has grown ever since.

The Events

There are five different Alpine events for men and for women. The best-known and most exciting, for spectators and TV viewers alike, is the downhill. Here the skier tries to record the fastest time during a single run down a steep slope with a minimum of turns.

Speeds in the downhill often exceed 60 miles an hour, and world-class downhill courses generally take about two minutes to complete. World records are less important in downhill than in most speed events, because conditions can vary so greatly from one course to the next and even from one day to the next. It is the best time on a particular day that counts.

The dangers of plunging down an icy slope at more than sixty miles an hour are obvious, and the downhill racer must display an extraordinary blend of strength, skill, and nerve to be successful.

The slalom is an event that requires the skier to make many short, quick turns through two different courses. Slalom is staged in two runs, and the times are added together to determine the final finish order. The men's slalom course is required to have between fifty-five and seventy-five "gates," which look like little colored flags mounted on a pair of flexible metal poles. The women's course has forty to sixty gates. The competitors are required to pass between all the gates in a predetermined order.

Giant slalom is an event that skiers believe requires the most technical skill. Skiers race down the mountain on a course that is faster and more open than in the slalom, but they are still required to go through a number of gates. The exact number of gates is determined by the nature of the course. Like sla-

Giant slalom (Photo by Nancie Battaglia)

lom, giant slalom is staged in two runs with the times added together to determine the final finish order.

Super giant, or super G, as it is called, was introduced into the Olympics at Calgary in 1988. Simply put, super G is a hybrid of downhill and giant slalom. Like downhill, the event is decided in a single run. Long sweeping high-speed turns make this event popular with spectators.

The combined event involves the combination of scores from designated downhill and slalom events.

The Olympics

Probably no single event more typifies the Winter Olympics than the men's downhill. The winner is catapulted to instant fame, often fortune, and sometimes controversy. Perhaps the greatest Alpine skier of the modern era was the handsome Frenchman Jean-Claude Killy. In 1968 Killy was favored to win the triple crown of Olympic Alpine skiing: the downhill, the slalom, and the giant slalom. If he did, he could expect to be asked to endorse many ski products for enormous sums of money. At that time, however, a nasty controversy was brewing between the French Ski Federation and Avery Brundage, the American head of the International Olympic Committee (IOC). Brundage, a fierce opponent of commercialism and professionalism in the games, was opposed to Killy's making money from his amateur contests. Many felt that Brundage was out of touch with the realities of modern athletics. Athletes needed to be able to support themselves. He had come from an era when most amateur athletes were "gentlemen of independent means" and didn't have to worry about money. Eventually a compromise was reached, and Killy did win the triple gold. Shortly thereafter he quit competitive skiing to become an extremely wealthy man by endorsing a variety of products from gloves to automobiles. His fame remains, particularly in France. The ski area in which the 1992 Olympic Alpine skiing will be held is named after him. Killy himself grew up in the resort village of Val-d'Isère.

Brundage announced that 1972 would be his final year as head of the IOC. But at the 1972 Winter Games in Sapporo, Japan, he launched one final attack on commercialism. He engineered an Olympic ban on Karl Schranz of Austria. Schranz was without doubt the best Alpine skier in the world and a clear favorite to win Olympic gold. But because he had received some relatively small amounts of money from ski manufacturers he was out of the games. The downhill winner that year was Bernhard Russi of Switzerland, an excellent athlete, but as far as the world, and particularly Austria, was concerned, Schranz was still number one. When Schranz returned to Vienna he received the biggest demonstration there since the end of World War II.

In 1976 the winner was Franz Klammer of Austria, who put on one of the wildest displays of downhill racing ever seen. "I thought I was going to crash all the way," said Klammer afterward. No one who saw his incredible run would have disagreed.

No U.S. Olympic skier had ever won a medal in the men's downhill until Bill Johnson won a gold in 1984 at Sarajevo. And, as seems to be traditional in the sport, the win was controversial. Bill Johnson was a very unlikely winner. At seventeen he had been arrested for stealing a car. Instead of prison he was sent to a ski academy. The sentence worked. He never stole another car, and he became a pretty good, though not outstanding, skier.

Because the conditions in 1984 favored Johnson's gliding style, he did win. Johnson, however, was not modest and quickly made enemies among the other competitors and the press. He denounced what he called the European "downhill mafia." When it was said that he won only because of the unusual circumstances, Johnson snapped, "If it's so easy, why didn't *they* win?"

The most impressive overall showing for American men in Alpine events came at Sarajevo when twins Phil and Steve Mahre took first and second in the slalom.

American women have done considerably better than the men in Olympic Alpine skiing, but historically they have not received much interest or publicity. Gretchen Fraser was the first American woman to win a medal in Olympic Alpine in 1948, when she won a gold in slalom. She complained, "Nobody paid any attention to us [the U.S. women's team]. The reporters never came over for any interviews. They said, 'Oh, if someone breaks a leg, let us know and we'll send that [story] home.' . . . But they didn't care about us."

What to Look For

While the U.S. ski team has been doing better in international Alpine competition, there are no sure bets or heavy favorites for Olympic medals among American skiers. As usual, Alpine skiing will probably be dominated by the Europeans. Injuries, snow conditions, and just plain luck can change the outcome of many of the events. The history of the Olympics is filled with stories of upsets and surprise finishes. As usual, the U.S. women's team appears to be stronger than the men's.

Be sure not to miss the downhill. It is the purest form of ski racing and, in the opinion of many, the most thrilling spectacle at any Winter Olympics.

For more information:

United States Ski Team
P.O. Box 100
1500 Kearns Blvd.
Park City, Ut 84060
(801) 649-9090

11

BOBSLED

History

Bobsledding, in which teams of two or four men fly down an ice covered track at breakneck speed, has long been considered one of the most dangerous of all sports in the Winter Olympics. Four-man bobsled races were part of the very first Winter Games. Two-man races were not held until the third Winter Games at Lake Placid in 1932. Bobsledding has remained one of the most popular spectator sports at the Winter Games.

The origins of this well-received sport are rather obscure, though. Nearly everyone who lives in a region where it snows regularly has ridden on a sled. Competitive sled racing has been popular in Europe for centuries, but the bobsled seems to have been a comparatively recent development. The Swiss resort towns of Saint Moritz and Davos both claim to be the birthplace of bobsled racing. In truth the bobsled is almost certainly an American development. The first "bobsled" used for sport was brought to Switzerland in the winter of 1888–89 by Stephen Whitney, a tourist from New York City. It consisted of two low "American" sleds connected by a board and held together with bolts. Whitney's sled was superior to local sleds when it was tested on the run at Davos. It reached a considerable speed and was described as "a very dangerous machine to drive."

We don't know where the idea for the first bobsled came from. Sleds of that general type existed in the United States as early as 1839; however, they were not used for racing, but for carrying wood. The earliest known photo of a bobsled shows one of these monsters in a carnival parade on a street in Albany, New York. These sleds were not well suited for sport, but they could be steered from the rear as well as from the front, and they apparently gave Whitney the idea for his bobsled. There are no known instances of bobsleds being used for sport in the United States at that early date. In fact, there was very little competitive sled racing in the United States at all.

According to legend, the earliest bobsleds had no brakes and were stopped by dragging a garden rake. The sled could be steered with a rope that turned the runners. At first bob-

Four-man bobsled (Photo by Nancie Battaglia)

sledding wasn't a team sport. Whitney and his imitators rode their one-man sleds lying down, head first. In luge, which is primarily a single-person sledding event, the athlete rides the sled lying on his or her back. Head-first sledding is a sport now known as skeleton. More about that shortly. The equipment for bobsledding developed very quickly. Within a year, two-seat and multiseat steel bobsleds were being raced at Saint Moritz. That's why both Davos and Saint Moritz claim to be the birthplace of bobsled racing. There was no fixed number of team members at first; three-man to six-man teams were treated equally.

The sport caught on very quickly. No sooner had bobsledding begun at Saint Moritz than other European winter resorts took up the idea. By 1911 there were about sixty bobsled runs in Switzerland alone. Most, however, were no more than a path on an ordinary street with snow-reinforced curves.

There were no particular rules about equipment until the 1920s. The usual apparel for men consisted of a thick woolen cap pulled down to expose only the eyes and nose to the cold, sweaters, elbow-length gloves, cuffs or leggings made of sailcloth or leather, and high hiking boots. Any adventurous woman who wanted to try this dangerous sport wore a long winter coat, high-top boots, a hood, or a broad-brimmed hat secured with a scarf. It was a long way to the aerodynamically designed rubberized suits worn by today's bobsledders.

Early bobsledding was pretty much a daredevil sport. There were few safety devices on the sleds. It wasn't until the 1920s that bobsledders even began wearing protective helmets, and these were primitive affairs made of compressed cardboard, leather, plywood, and other materials. Helmets did not become regulation until the 1930s. Elbows and knees were protected by leather or felt pads.

The United States Bobsled Federation admits: "It is a sad fact that accidents are as old as bobsledding itself and are a black page in its history. Of small comfort is the fact that it is the accidents that have led to stricter safety regulations in the sport. Every athlete chooses his sport himself, with full awareness of the risks." The federation feels that the myriad regulations and the improvements in the course and the equipment "have made contemporary bobsledding very safe, yet the sport has lost nothing of its high speed thrill."

Modern bobsledding certainly is safer than it has ever been. But like downhill skiing and high diving, it presents a genuine element of risk as well. It is the speed and the danger that attract certain athletes to take up the sport, however, and that make it such a heart-pounding spectacle to watch.

Canada's four-man bobsled (Photo by Nancie Battaglia)

Sleds and Tracks

Though a bobsled may appear to be jet propelled as it shoots down the track, its only sources of propulsion are human muscle and gravity. All things being equal, the heaviest sled-crew combination should run the fastest. Therefore there is a maximum weight set for each sled. Four-man sleds cannot exceed 1,388 pounds, and two-man sleds cannot exceed 859 pounds. Lighter crews can add weight to their sleds during a race. But extra weight can also create problems. Bobsled racers depend on an explosive start to give them the momentum to carry them down the track. The race starts with the sled at a dead stop. The team begins outside the sled, pushes like mad to get it moving, and then jumps in for the ride. Speeds are slowest at the start of the race when they are most important. Racers who beat a competitor's time by a second at the beginning of a race can finish up to three seconds faster at the bottom. Heavier sleds are more difficult to start. Thus adding weight to a sled for competition can actually work against a lighter bobsled team. A big strong crew, which has the power to give the sled the needed explosion at the start and the weight to carry it swiftly to the finish, is considered best.

Numerous very technical and specific rules govern the size and shape of the sled. In international competition like the Olympics there are only tiny variations between the different sleds, and winning is most often determined by the skill of the team rather than by any innovations in equipment. Part of a team's skill is determining how to prepare a sled's steel runners for optimum speed for the temperature and ice conditions on the day of the race.

Steering and maintaining a straight downhill line are also critical elements in winning races. Bobsleds are steered by a rope-and-pulley system. The drivers barely have to move the ropes to affect the direction of the sled. Changing the direction of a sled, even slightly, will slow it down, so the less steering the drivers do, the faster the sled will go. The best results come when a crew remains as still as possible and the driver lets the sled do the work. The downhill line of the sled is also important; straight lines yield the best results. Sleds can lose a tremendous amount of speed at the top of a race by merely bumping into a wall. This translates into slower times for the entire race. Remember, a bobsled isn't a race car. The driver can't press down on any pedals to give it more power. Once the momentum is lost, it's lost for the whole race. While maintaining the straightest possible line down the course, drivers also try not to let their sleds rock from side to side when coming out of curves. A sled that appears to shoot cleanly out of a curve is the one that will probably post the fastest finishing time. A sled that rocks or bumps the wall is losing precious time.

The construction of a bobsled track, or run, for international competition is also subject to an enormous number of rules. Bobsled runs used in international competition are approximately one mile in length. In many sports, tracks are constructed to maximize speed, but in bobsledding many of the rules governing the construction of tracks are aimed at keeping the speed of the sleds down for safety reasons. Careful attention is paid to construction of the curves, the most dangerous portions of any bobsled track. A curve must be designed so that it will be impossible for a sled to exceed a force greater than 4Gs (four times the force of gravity) during a period greater than three seconds.

The Olympics

There was a four-man bobsled race in the first Winter Olympics at Chamonix in 1924. The two-man sleds didn't appear in Olympic competition until the 1932 games at Lake Placid. American teams dominated the early years of Olympic bobsledding, but in recent years leadership has passed to the Europeans, who have put more time and money into developing and training world-class bobsled teams. Bobsledding is an expensive and time-consuming sport. Few individuals are wealthy enough to be able to field their own bobsled team.

Throughout the history of the Winter Games the events have been plagued by poor weather. In 1932, 1936, and 1968 bobsled races were disrupted by the weather. At the 1932 games in Lake Placid the four-man bobsled was delayed until after the official closing ceremony, and even then conditions were so dangerous that many of the competitors refused to race. The event had to be rescheduled. In 1968 at Grenoble, the threat of a sudden thaw forced officials to limit the contest to two runs instead of the usual four.

Since competitive bobsledding is carried out at the edge of disaster, both the officials and the bobsledders are very concerned about weather, which can drastically alter the conditions of the track. There have been many spectacular accidents in Olympic bobsledding, but fortunately no deaths. Felix Endrich, who won the gold medal as part of the two-man Swiss bobsled team in 1948, was killed a few years later while racing on a four-man bobsled team.

Bobsledding is one sport in which athletes do not have to be young to compete. In 1956 the Italian team of Lamberto Dalla Costa and Giacomo Conti won the gold in the two-man bobsled. Dalla Costa was a thirty-five-year-old jet pilot with no real experience in international bobsled racing. Conti, at age forty-seven, became the oldest person ever to win a gold medal at the Winter Olympics.

In 1932 American Eddie Eagan, a member of the four-man bobsled team, became the first person to have won a gold medal in both the Summer and the Winter Olympics. In 1920 he had won the light heavyweight boxing championship at the Summer Games in Antwerp, Belgium. Eagan was part of an unusual team. The driver on his bobsled team was Billy Fiske, regarded as the boy wonder of bobsledding. He had led a U.S. team to the gold in 1928 when he was only sixteen! When World War II broke out, Fiske was the first American to join the British Royal Air Force. He died as the result of wounds received over Germany in 1939. Another member of that team was forty-year-old Clifford ''Tippy'' Gray, a songwriter, whose three thousand songs included ''Got a Date with an Angel'' and ''If You Were the Only Girl in the World.'' It was said that Gray was such a modest man that not even his children knew he had won two Olympic gold medals until after he died.

The man to watch this year is Edwin Moses, a member of the U.S. two-man Olympic bobsledding team. Moses has already won two gold medals in hurdling at the Summer Games, and is considered not only the greatest hurdler of all time but one of the truly great athletes of the modern era. Moses remained a virtually unbeatable hurdler until well into his thirties. When this highly competitive athlete felt that he could no longer remain in the top rank of hurdlers, he switched to bobsledding and quickly became one of the best in that sport. If the U.S. two-man team takes a gold in 1992, and Moses competes, he will become only the second man to have won the gold in both the Summer and the Winter Games.

A big crowd and media favorite at the 1988 Winter Olympics was the bobsled team from Jamaica. They didn't win any medals and weren't expected to. What made them unusual was that their home is a tropical island where it never snows! The team did its basic training on a bobsled on wheels rather than runners. They had to come to the United States to get experience on ice.

What to Watch For

In both two- and four-man bobsledding each team makes four runs, and the total time of the four runs determines the winner. Consistency is vital.

Most bobsledders say that the race is won or lost at the start. This is where teamwork really counts. All members of the team must push together and then jump cleanly into the sled. A sled that bumps the sides of the run or takes

Four-man bobsled, push start (Photo by Nancie Battaglia)

the curves at too high or too low an angle is losing time and probably losing the race.

Keep in mind that weather is an important consideration in bobsledding. The artificial refrigerated run for bobsled and luge at the Alpine winter resort complex of La Roche is an excellent facility and should be immune to all but the most severe of sudden thaws, but there is still the possibility of heavy snow or heavy fog. These could cause events to be postponed or canceled, and the weather in this area can be unreliable.

Skeleton Racing

The national governing body for bobsledding in the United States is the United States Bobsled & Skeleton Federation. Skeleton is not what you might think. It is a small racing sled on which a man or a woman races down a bobsled run, protected only by a helmet, elbow pads, and skill. Luge also uses a bobsled run and is normally a single event, but in luge the slider is on his or her back, whereas in skeleton the ride is taken head first, the way most of us first rode a sled down a hill.

Today skeleton is barely known as a sport, yet it was probably the first sliding sport, with races recorded in the nineteenth century. The first bobsled was really little more than two skeletons tied together. Skeleton was an Olympic sport in the past, but it became eclipsed by bobsled and luge.

There will be no skeleton races at the Albertville Olympics, but the U.S. Federation and some other bobsled organizations are making a powerful push to bring skeleton back as an Olympic sport in the near future. It is already being tried out in some non-Olympic international competitions. The inevitable slogan is "Skeleton is back, make no bones about it." The argument is that since it costs millions to build a track for just two events— luge and bobsled—adding a third could be a money-maker for organizers of future Olympic games. It is also a relatively inexpensive sport to compete in: about $1,000 for a sled, $125 for a helmet, and $125 for a rubber speed suit. Compare that to the cost of a bobsled, which can run between $12,000 and $25,000. Skeleton racing now takes place at the bobsled track in Lake Placid, and there are plans to build another track, in Salt Lake City, Utah, which will open the sport to sliders from the West.

The headquarters for bobsled and skeleton is still Lake Placid. If you are there during the right season you might be able to arrange a passenger ride on a bobsled. Call ahead for details.

For more information:

United States Bobsled & Skeleton Federation
P.O. Box 828
Lake Placid, NY 12946
(518) 523-1842

12

LUGE

History

In the famous movie *Citizen Kane* the dying newspaper tycoon, Charles Foster Kane, utters his last word. It is "Rosebud." No one knows what the word means. Much of the film centers around trying to discover the meaning of this word. It turns out that Rosebud is the name of the little wooden sled that Kane had when he was a child. It is a symbol of his lost innocence.

At one time or another most of us have probably owned a sled that looked like Rosebud. Of course, sled runners are now made of metal rather than wood, but the basic shape remains the same. And most of us can probably also remember at one time or another sliding down a snowy hill at what seemed like breakneck speed, trying desperately to control the little sled without tipping over or crashing into a tree.

The word "luge" may be unfamiliar to you. But if you have done what we have just described, then you have participated in luge, at least in a primitive form. "Luge" comes from a word meaning "sled" in the dialect of the Alpine region of southern France.

Until fairly recently people in the United States were pretty much content to slide down local snow-covered hills on the equivalent of Rosebud. In Europe, though, sledding has been a much more serious and competitive sport for centuries.

The first references to competitive sledding appear in medieval Norwegian chronicles. By the eighteenth century the people of the old Russian capital, Saint Petersburg, were riding down artificially constructed ice hills. In 1881 a Swiss resort organized the first international luge race. There were Americans among the competitors, but the sport never caught on in the United States. In fact, before the luge was inaugurated at the Innsbruck Olympic Winter Games in 1964, few Americans had ever even heard of the sport.

In the early years of Olympic competition, the United States did enter a luge team, but there was no formal luge program in the United States. The U.S. Olympic Luge Team consisted mainly of American soldiers who had taken the sport up when they were posted

U.S. national luge team member Cammy Myler (U.S. Luge Assn.)

in Europe. Back in the United States there were a few athletes who had an interest in the sport, but there was no luge track. American sliders—that's what those who ride the luge are called—had to practice on the Olympic bobsled run, built in Lake Placid, New York, in 1932.

In 1980 the Winter Olympics returned to Lake Placid, and that required the construction of the nation's first and only refrigerated luge run. That same year the U.S. Luge Association was formed as the sport's national governing body.

Since then a national network of luge teams has developed. Although the Lake Placid course remains the only luge run in the United States accredited for international competition, three other luge tracks have been built or are currently under construction in the United States.

For most Americans luge remains a curiosity. The United States cannot realistically expect any gold medals in luge at the 1992 Winter Olympics. Traditional favorites in this event are Germany, Italy, and Austria. However, American sliders have picked up some medals in international competition in recent years. While the United States is certainly not one of the international powerhouses in this sport, the days are gone when American sliders always finished last.

In Olympic competition there are luge races

for men and women, and a doubles event for men. The women and the doubles run a slightly shorter course than the men's singles, but otherwise the rules for men and women are the same.

The Science of Luge

Though its origins are simple, modern luge is probably more dependent on technology than any other sport in the Winter Games. The sled isn't Rosebud anymore. With modern racing technology a sled today can reach a speed of 80 miles per hour. Four factors influence the speed of a luge sled on the track: weight, air resistance, friction, and the slider's driving ability.

A luge sled must conform to very specific regulations regarding weight and size. In singles the sled cannot weigh more than 48.4 pounds (22 kilograms). In doubles the sled weight can be no more than 55 pounds (25 kilograms).

Heavier drivers generally have an advantage in that gravity pulls their sleds down more quickly. To overcome this, lighter drivers can add extra weight, usually in the form of a weighted vest. Like jockeys at a racetrack, luge drivers are weighed at the end of each race to make sure that they are carrying only the weight they are allowed.

Luge doubles (Photo by Nancie Battaglia)

The sled itself is designed as an aerodynamic racing platform. It has wooden, fiberglass, or plastic runners that support hardened steel blades. A thin rubber pad cushions the slider, who rides on a fiberglass "seat." It's something of a misnomer, for the slider sits only briefly at the start of the run. The seat is also, and more accurately, called the "pod." Small metal handles near the front of the sled provide a stabilizing grip.

The runners are slanted so that only a few inches of the blade actually come in contact with the ice. Heated blades could unfairly improve luge speed, and runner temperatures are measured before and after each run to prevent cheating. In the 1968 Winter Olympics East German women were disqualified for heating the runners on their sleds. Other luge teams threatened to walk out if any East Germans competed. The International Luge Federation decided against suspending the East German men, but the competition was halted because of bad weather, so the controversy ended without a formal walkout.

Lugers are absolutely fanatic about preparing their blades for a race. The course and the weather conditions dictate the best edge for a fast run. For very cold ice a sharp blade is best, and when the weather is warmer a slightly duller edge prevents blades from digging in and slowing the ride. Blades are honed by each slider or coach before every race.

People viewing luge for the first time are always struck by how odd it looks. The slider goes down the run flat on his or her back, feet first. Everything possible is done to cut air resistance. That's why, once the run has started, the slider stretches out on his or her back on the sled. Steering is done with body movements: pressure of the legs on the front runners and pressure of the shoulders on the back of the seat.

Because the slider covers most of the sled while riding it, he or she must be able to slice through the air as easily as possible. To do this the luge athlete wears a specially designed skintight rubberized suit, pointed racing shoes, and a rounded protective helmet with a clear face mask. There are no exposed buttons, zippers, or decorations. The object of this high-tech uniform is to minimize clothing wrinkles that might catch the wind, increase drag, and slow the rider.

The only exception to this entirely smooth uniform is the gloves, which have spiked knuckles or palms. To start the sled down the run the slider must push off, and the spikes provide a grip on the ice for a more explosive start. Once the race starts, the sliders tuck their gloved hands securely inside the pod.

So vital is aerodynamic form that Olympic contenders often try out their positions and equipment in a wind tunnel. Sensors measure the flow of air across the body and sled. This

Using the spiked gloves to push-start in luge (Photo by Nancie Battaglia)

helps the rider find the very best position for legs, elbows, head, and torso.

If you've ever worn a visor or face mask in cold weather, you know that fogging is a real problem. Before a race, sliders carefully wipe the insides of their masks with antifogging preparations. The contents of these preparations are a closely guarded secret. The mask goes over the face only at the last moment before takeoff.

The Slider

Experienced sliders say that most races are won or lost at the start. These athletes need tremendous upper body strength for the explosive push-off. Neck muscles also have to be exceptionally strong to withstand pressures as great as three or four times the force of gravity in turns.

If the luge run were dead straight, the slider wouldn't have to steer at all and the sled would go faster, because any steering action tends to slow the sled a bit. A normal luge run, which includes many curves, requires the driver to steer about 70 percent of the time.

Using the legs is the quickest and most powerful way to steer a sled. The slider presses down on the end of the runner with his leg. The problem with leg steering is that it causes the greatest loss of speed. A more desirable,

Testing luge equipment in a wind tunnel (U.S. Luge Assn.)

but less powerful method, is to steer the luge by pressing down with the shoulders. Subtle pressure can also be applied by rolling the head from side to side.

Flat on their backs and traveling at 70 miles an hour or more, the sliders have a hard time keeping a view of the track. "Losing your head" means losing visual contact with the track, a dangerous situation that is sure to throw off a slider's timing and can even make it necessary to abort a run. Sliders must have a good mental picture of the course so as to be able to respond within a fraction of a second to all the twists, turns, and drops. An average luge run takes between forty and fifty-five seconds.

Men's doubles competition looks even more bizarre than singles competition. Here two sliders are jammed on top of what appears to be a ridiculously tiny sled. In such a situation teamwork is everything.

Both men must pull together for a quick start and then lie back to cut the air resistance. The increased weight of a doubles team raises the potential for speed, but it also creates more friction on the runners and greater wind resistance.

The top man has a clear view of the track and handles the runners. His partner, who can't see much at all, takes his cue from the top man, applying shoulder pressure to complete the turn.

The end of a luge run is particularly exciting. Sliders must come to a quick stop. They do so by sitting up, grasping the curved portions of their runners, and lifting up to dig in the backs of the blades. Their feet serve as runners during this maneuver, and the athletes are often obscured by a cloud of flying snow and ice chips.

What to Watch For

Luge is an exciting sport to watch. Those who watch the Games on television have a better view of the races than do those who see them in person. In Albertville there will be cameras at several spots, whereas a spectator will be able to see only a small portion of the race.

Since the typical run lasts under a minute you have to watch very carefully. Tenths, even hundredths, of a second may separate the finishers. Tiny errors cost fractions of a second, which can mean the difference between finishing with a medal and being listed as an also-ran. A smooth and powerful motion pulling through the starting gate is all-important. The sliders then paddle the ice with their spiked gloves to pick up speed, and lie back in the racing position to fly through the first turn.

Experienced lugers say that relaxation is the

key to a good run. A rigid, tense body tends to telegraph sled action down to the blades, causing them to dig in and reduce speed. In a relaxed position, the slider absorbs vibrations, keeping the blades on the ice and improving control and speed.

The contender who appears to be making the least effort is usually the one who comes out with the best time. Those who are out of position on their sleds and seem to be working hard are probably in trouble and falling behind.

The sliders want to enter and leave each turn at precisely the right height. All contenders keep in mind an imaginary line which they try to follow down the course. By entering a turn too high the slider wastes time. Entering too low cuts momentum. A driver who loops back and forth coming out of a turn has overcorrected and is losing precious fractions of a second.

There are crashes, when the driver completely loses control of the sled and flips over. Luge looks dangerous, and at a highly competitive level it can be. There have been several injuries and at least one death in Olympic luge, though these occurred in the early days. The International Luge Racing Federation has worked to make the sport as safe as possible.

The United States Luge Association runs a small number of programs for people who are interested in getting involved with the sport. Introductory programs are held on a regular basis. Because it takes a long time to develop internationally competitive lugers, coaches are particularly interested in younger athletes, from twelve to sixteen years of age.

For more information write or call:

United States Luge Association
P.O. Box 651
Lake Placid, NY 12946
(518) 523-2071

13

BIATHLON

History

Biathlon is probably the least known of all the medal-awarding sports at the Winter Olympics. It is a competition that involves both Nordic (cross-country) skiing and target shooting. The word "biathlon" is Greek in origin and it means "two tests." Biathlon is most similar to the modern pentathlon of the Summer Games. The pentathlon is a test of five different skills including horseback riding and pistol shooting. As you might have guessed both of these events are military in origin.

Despite its obscurity the biathlon is quite an old sport. The first documented competition in biathlon was held in 1767 along the border between Sweden and Norway, between ski runner companies guarding the border.

Ninety-four years later, in 1861, the world's first recorded shooting and ski club, the Trysil

Rifle and Ski Club was formed in Norway to encourage national defense. Competitions in biathlon have been held continuously ever since.

Biathlon was a demonstration sport at the first Olympic Winter Games in 1924. It was then known as the military patrol. It was dropped after the 1948 Olympics because of the antimilitary sentiment in Europe that resulted from World War II. But the sport made a comeback in 1960 as a regular Olympic event, and since that time it has been expanded from one to three events: the 20-kilometer (12.4 mile) individual, the 10-kilometer (6.2 mile) sprint, and the 4 x 7.5-kilometer (4.7 mile) relay. Each member of a four-man team skis 7.5 kilometers. Traditionally biathlon has been a men's-only event, but in the 1980s more and more women began competing in the sport. In 1984 the first Women's World Championships were held in Chamonix, France. In the 1992 games women's biathlon will be a medal sport for the first time in Olympic history. The women will run a slightly shorter course than the men, but otherwise the rules will be the same.

Since biathlon was reintroduced into Olympic competition the sport has been dominated by the Soviet Union, Sweden, Norway, Finland, and Germany. The United States has regularly fielded a team, but has never been a power.

Biathlon (Sports File, Scott Smith)

Scoring

Biathlon is basically a race against the clock. Competitors start by skiing a prescribed distance. Next, they shoot at five targets from either a prone or a standing position. Then they ski another leg, then shoot again. The individual or the team with the least elapsed time wins. There is a catch: the competitor must also hit the target. In individual competitions, a one-minute penalty is added to the skiing time for every miss. In the sprint events, the competitor has to ski an extra penalty loop for each target missed. The time it takes to ski around the penalty loop or the one-minute penalty is then added to the final skiing time.

There are minor individual variations in the way the different events are run. A difference between the individual races and the relay is that competitors in the individual events have only five shots at the five targets while in the relay, the athletes can take eight shots at the five targets. Extra shots take extra seconds, but completely missing one of the targets results in a penalty, which is much more costly in time.

Range Procedure

Neither the strongest skier nor the most accurate shooter necessarily wins this event. The real skill lies in being able to make the switch smoothly between these two very different activities. The competition can be won or lost on what the athletes call *range procedure*. That is the time it takes to enter the firing range, unsling the rifle, load it, shoot five rounds, resling the rifle, and exit the range. Competitors try to make these moves in the shortest time possible.

While skiing, the competitors have to maintain a high intensity of energy, somewhere around 90 percent of maximum effort. During this period the athlete's heart is beating 170 to 190 times a minute.

Skiing requires tremendous exertion. Shooting, on the other hand, requires calm and steadiness. As the athletes approach the range—the place where the targets are set up—they reduce their skiing speed slightly to slow their breathing in preparation for shooting. Ideally they try to lower their pulse rate to about 150 beats a minute for each shooting segment.

Once they reach the firing point, the athletes loosen one strap so that their rifles hang on their right shoulders. Then they plant their ski poles and assume the shooting position, either standing or prone. Then the contestants load their rifles, gather their composure and concentration, and fire five rounds at approximately five-second intervals. After firing the last shot, they sling their rifles on their backs and continue into the next skiing segment or loop. Depending on the skill of the athlete, it takes anywhere from twenty-five seconds to one minute to complete the range procedure. Olympic-class biathletes average approximately thirty seconds on the range.

Because the two skills are so different, the winner is not the fastest skier or the most accurate marksman, but the competitor who has the best combination of the two skills.

The event makes enormous physical demands on the athletes. In 1968 Magnar Solbereg a thirty-one-year-old police officer from Norway was the surprise winner of the 20-kilometer event. As photographers crowded around the surprised champion, he told them, "I am very happy, but too tired to smile."

What to Watch For

There probably will not be much live coverage of the biathlon, and U.S. viewers will see mainly taped segments. However, here are some tips on watching the event.

The relay competition is the easiest to follow. All teams start simultaneously and ski the same course. The fastest skiers emerge from the course first, and the weaker shooters spend more time at the range and in the penalty loop. Each team consists of four skiers. There is a tag zone where each skier, when completing his or her segment of the relay, touches the next teammate to start. The first team across the finish line is the winner.

The sprint competition requires the athletes to ski hard because of the short distance (10 kilometers for men and 7.5 kilometers for women), but they must remain calm at the range. Each miss means a penalty loop, which can really hurt the overall timing. Spectators should remember that the athletes are shooting only once in each of the positions, prone and standing. The winner is the athlete with the fastest time.

The individual competition is the most physically demanding. A 20-kilometer event for the men and a 15-kilometer race for the women, the individual competition requires the athletes to pace themselves, saving energy for the final ski loop. This event involves more range action, with no penalty loops skied, and is exciting for you, as a spectator, toward the end of the race as you wait to see who will remain calm enough to shoot well. The winner is the athlete with the fastest skiing time in combination with the fewest penalty minutes assessed for missed targets.

115

GOING FOR THE GOLD

For more information:

United States Biathlon Association
P.O. Box 5515
Essex Junction, VT 05453

14

DEMONSTRATION SPORTS

Not all the sports at the Olympic Games are recognized medal-awarding Olympic sports. At every Olympiad, Winter and Summer, there are demonstration sports. These are events that are being considered as Olympic sports and are given a tryout to see how well they fit into the Olympics. Some demonstration sports quickly become recognized Olympic events, others remain demonstration sports for many years, and some simply fade away.

The main requirement of a demonstration sport is that it be played in many different countries, so that there can be true international competition. American-style football, for example, would not make a good Olympic sport. It is extraordinarily popular in the United States, but is played practically nowhere else in the world.

At the 1992 Winter Games there will be three demonstration events: curling, speed skiing, and freestyle skiing.

CURLING

The first time you watch a curling match you are likely to be both puzzled and amused. Here are men and women sliding large (up to 44-pound) rocks or stones over the ice. Two players run frantically in front of the sliding stone, sweeping the ice with brooms. It's the brooms that stick in the mind and make the sport look funny.

What's going on? A little history will help. Curling is an old game. It originated in sixteenth-century Scotland. Winters were long and cold, and the facilities for outdoor recreation were limited. The Scots amused themselves by sliding big stones across the surface of frozen ponds and lochs. Occasionally the ice was a bit too thin, creating more excitement than expected.

The original curling stones were just large stones that had been formed by nature. They often curved, or curled, as they slid across the ice—hence the name "curling." Originally the brooms were used to clear snow from the path of the stone. Curling was a fairly primitive sport in those days.

In the eighteenth century Scottish immigrants brought the game with them to North America, where it spread across the northern United States and Canada. By 1855 there were curling clubs in New York City, Detroit, Milwaukee, and Portage, Wisconsin. While curling has always had its devotees in the United States, it has been more popular in Canada where, next to ice hockey, it is considered something of a national sport.

The game has evolved and changed in many ways. It can still be played outdoors, but most modern games are played on indoor rinks with refrigerated ice. The stones are specially made from dense granite quarried in Wales. They have metal handles that make it easier for the players to slide them over the ice. Even the brooms are specially made so as not to scratch the ice.

There are two teams of four players each. The object of the game is to shoot, deliver, or slide stones along the playing surface—called, appropriately enough, "a sheet of ice"—into the "house" of the opposing team. The score is determined by which team gets the most stones close to the center of a 12-foot circle.

While one player shoots, two sweep. The

sweeping is no longer necessary to clear the snow from the ice, but it does polish the ice so that the stone will travel farther. Vigorous sweeping takes a lot of energy. In a typical game a curler walks about two miles.

All four team members shoot two stones at each "end," or inning, and sweep for their teammates' shots. Games have eight to ten ends and usually last from two to two and a half hours.

The captain of each team is called the "skip." (By now you've gathered that curling has its own jargon.) It is the skip who determines the strategy for the team. Curling involves much more than simply sliding a hunk of granite over the ice. A lot of real strategy is used. For example, sometimes a rock can't score, but it is placed in such a way that it "guards" the scoring rock. Strategy sometimes becomes so complicated that curling has been called "chess on ice."

Men's and women's curling is still a demonstration sport for men and women at the Olympics. It first appeared as a demonstration sport in the 1988 Winter Olympiad. Curling's future as a fully recognized Olympic event is unknown. But in some respects curling fulfills, almost perfectly, one of the early ideals of the Olympics. Unlike figure skating, hockey, and Alpine skiing, curling is truly an amateur sport. There are well over a million curlers in Canada, Australia, New Zealand, Japan, and many Euro-

Curling (*North American Curling News*)

pean countries. There are curling clubs in twenty-three states in the United States. There is real international competition, but there are no professional curling teams. No curler, no matter how skilled, can expect to make a living at his sport. It is played strictly for love of the game.

Curling is an inexpensive sport to play. A pair of curling shoes and a broom are the only special equipment most curlers possess, and the novice can get along with ordinary athletic shoes and a broom lent by the local curling club. It's an easy sport to learn, though learning to play well takes experience. Since curling lacks the competitive intensity of higher-profile sports, curling clubs have the reputation of being exceptionally friendly and accepting.

Be sure to catch any TV coverage of this unique sport at the Olympics. Don't be put off by those funny-looking brooms. Then if you're interested in finding out more about the sport, or actually trying curling yourself here is the group to contact:

> United States Curling Association
> 1100 Center Point Drive
> Box 971
> Stevens Point, WI 54481

SPEED SKIING

This event is exactly what its name implies—a sport in which the athletes try to ski as fast as possible. Like speed skaters, swimmers, and track and field competitors, speed skiers try not only to win but also to break world records. Since this is a relatively new event, world records fall regularly. There will be demonstrations of both men's and women's speed skiing.

In one form or another, speed skiing has been around for over a century. But it wasn't until 1988 that the International Ski Federation assumed the responsibility for sanctioning speed skiing events throughout the world and brought enough order to the sport to make it a viable demonstration event.

A speed skiing track contains three segments: the inrun, the trap, and the outrun. The inrun is a steep course where the competitors build speed, the (speed) trap is a 100-meter section placed where the competitors carry the greatest momentum and thus the

Speed skiing (Sports File, Bob Allen)

greatest speed, and the outrun is the deceleration and transition segment that gradually slows the competitors to a controlled stop. Because of the enormous speeds, this is potentially a dangerous sport, and speed skiers wear distinctive protective helmets.

How fast do speed skiers go? Speeds of 100 miles an hour are common. A recent men's record set by Michael Prufer of Monaco was 139.03 miles an hour. At the time, the women's record, held by Tarja Mulari of Finland was 133.259 miles an hour. The Olympic demonstration will be held at the Alpine resort of Les Arcs-Bourg-Saint-Maurice, where the current speed skiing world record was set.

Speed skiing devotees believe that the exposure the sport will get at the Olympics will increase popularity enormously. It is certainly going to be an exciting event to watch.

The sport has recently formulated a point system that allows comparisons to be made between speeds achieved at world record tracks and those made on slower courses. World record speeds will always be the goal, but specific sites will be deemphasized as points become used.

For more information:

United States Ski Team
P.O. Box 100
1500 Kearns Blvd.
Park City, UT 84060
(801) 649-9090

FREESTYLE SKIING

Freestyle skiing requires skiing ability, extraordinary grace, and an almost daredevil attitude toward physical danger. It is also spectacular and bound to be enormously popular both with the spectators at the new Longnan stadium at Tignes and with the millions who will see the event on television.

There are several types of freestyle skiing for both men and women. The one that is sure to attract the most attention is the aerials. This is a sport that can more easily be compared to diving and gymnastics than to conventional skiing.

Freestyle has a checkered history. When freestyle skiing first appeared on the slopes it was called "hotdogging" and was regarded as a rowdy, semioutlaw, and unnecessarily dangerous activity. Still, it was popular, and there were a couple of professional freestyle cir-

Freestyle aerialist Lloyd Langlois of Canada (Photo by Nancie Battaglia)

cuits. During the 1970s freestyle was nearly torn apart by dissension. There were lots of lawsuits, filed mainly by athletes who had been seriously injured while performing certain aerial maneuvers. For a time some of these maneuvers were actually banned. In recent years there has been more control in the sport, and while it is still undoubtedly dangerous, it is not nearly so dangerous as it was in the early days.

Here's why freestyle is dangerous. The skiers take acrobatic leaps off specially prepared jumps. They are scored by five judges on the maneuvers they perform in the air and on the landing. The scores of the judges are multiplied by the degree of difficulty of the maneuver. The high and low scores are discarded.

All competitors take two jumps, and two types of maneuvers can be performed—inverted or upright. In an upright maneuver the competitor's head is never lower than his or her feet. This is not an aerial flip. The inverted maneuver is an aerial flip, and it's the most sensational of all freestyle maneuvers. In some competitions inverted aerials are performed as separate events. Everyone connected with freestyle skiing stresses that novices should not attempt this sort of maneuver. It takes a great deal of skill and training and can be dangerous even for experts. Like a high-wire performance at a circus, freestyle aerials are to be watched and admired by the crowd, but not

Freestyle world champion Kristie Marshell (Sports File, Lee Wardle)

imitated. The inverted aerials were the maneuvers that produced so many serious injuries during the early days of the sport. They don't look easy, and they're not.

The second event, freestyle ballet can be compared to figure skating on skis. The competitor performs a program of choreographed jumps, spins, and gliding steps within a predetermined area. The program is limited to two minutes and is accompanied by music of the competitor's choice. There is no set pattern the competitor must follow during the performance.

The competitor's performance is scored by seven judges. (Sometimes only five judges are available, but in the Olympics there will be seven.) The routine will be judged on composition, style, and technical difficulty. The high and low scores are discarded.

The third freestyle event is called moguls. A mogul is a small snow hill or bump. The event consists of carefully calculated high-speed turns down a slope dotted with moguls. Speed counts in this event, but so do form and style. Seven judges score the event.

There are winners in each of the freestyle events, and there is a combined winner—the athlete who has competed and placed highest overall in the three events.

Freestyle skiing first became popular in North America, and U.S. competitors have won most international competitions in this relatively new sport. The United States is expect-

Freestyle moguls (Photo © Dave Black)

ed to do very well at the Olympics, but no one is being complacent. The official U.S. ski team guide quotes a couple of old expressions: "Today's hero is tomorrow's zero," and "You're only as good as your last five minutes."

For more information contact:

United States Ski Team
P.O. Box 100
1500 Kearns Blvd.
Park City, UT 84060
(801) 649-9090

ABOUT THE AUTHORS

DANIEL COHEN is the author of more than a hundred books for young readers and adults. SUSAN COHEN is the author of several gothic novels and mysteries. The Cohens have coauthored a wide range of books for children and teenagers including *Heroes of the Challenger, Rock Video Superstars I* and *II, Wrestling Superstars I* and *II, Young and Famous: Sports' Newest Superstars,* and *Going for the Gold: Medal Hopefuls for Winter '92,* all of which are available in Archway Paperback editions.

Daniel Cohen is a former managing editor of *Science Digest* magazine and has a degree in journalism from the University of Illinois. Susan Cohen holds a master's degree in social work from Adelphi University. Both grew up in Chicago, where they married, later moving to New York. Today they live in Port Jervis, New York.